The Way Meat Loves Salt

A Cinderella Tale from the Jewish Tradition

Nina Jaffe

illustrated by Louise August

Henry Holt and Company

New York

Pronunciation Guide to Yiddish Names and Words in the Story

In Yiddish the letters *KH* are pronounced like *CH*, as in the name of the composer Johann Sebastian Bach.

These spellings and pronunciations are according to the YIVO standard of Yiddish-English transliteration, with the exception of the use of the final "h." "Hallah" and "huppah" are in accordance with common usage English spelling of these Hebrew words.

Reyzeleh	(RAY-zeh-leh)	badkhn	(BAHD-khen)
Khaveleh	(KHAH-veh-leh)	tsedokeh	(tseh-DOH-keh)
Mireleh	(MEE-reh-leh)	mazel tov	(MAH-zel tov)
Yitskhok ben Levi	(YITS-khok ben LEH-vee)		

The author is grateful to the staff at YIVO Institute for Jewish Research in New York City for consulting and the review of details in the text, pronunciation guide, and story—with thanks to Chana Mlotek, musicologist; Zachary Baker, head librarian; Dina Abramowitzc, librarian; and especially Beatrice Silverman Weinreich, senior research associate and the editor of *Yiddish Folktales*. The archives and library at YIVO are a precious resource and link to the living and vibrant culture of the Jews of eastern Europe, where this story was first told and collected.

Henry Holt and Company, Inc., *Publishers since 1866*, 115 West 18th Street, New York, New York 10011
Henry Holt is a registered trademark of Henry Holt and Company, Inc.
Text copyright © 1998 by Nina Jaffe. Illustrations copyright © 1998 by Louise August.
Song copyright © 1984 by the Hebrew University of Jerusalem. All rights reserved.
Published in Canada by Fitzhenry & Whiteside Ltd., 195 Allstate Parkway, Markham, Ontario L3R 4T8.

Library of Congress Cataloging-in-Publication Data
Jaffe, Nina.
The way meat loves salt: a Cinderella tale from the Jewish tradition / Nina Jaffe; illustrated by Louise August.
Summary: In this Eastern European Jewish variant of the Cinderella story, the youngest daughter of a rabbi is sent away from home in disgrace, but thanks to the help of the prophet Elijah, marries the son of a renowned scholar and is reunited with her family. Includes words and music to a traditional Yiddish wedding song.
[1. Jews—folklore. 2. Folklore—Europe, Eastern.] I. August, Louise, ill. II. Cinderella. English. III. Title.
PZ8.1.J156Way 1998 398.2'089'924—dc21 [E] 97-41286

ISBN 0-8050-4384-5 / First Edition—1998
The art for this book was prepared as linocuts painted in full-color oils on rice paper.
Printed in the United States of America on acid-free paper.∞
10 9 8 7 6 5 4 3

The song "Mazel Tov" from *Anthology of Yiddish Folksongs Vol. II* (1984) by Aharon Vinkovetzky, Abba Kovner, and Sinai Leichter is reprinted courtesy of Mount Scopus Publications by the Magnes Press, Hebrew University of Jerusalem.

Author's Note

The Cinderella tale is known around the world. It has countless variations documented throughout Europe, the Middle East, India, and West Africa. The earliest version of a Cinderella tale was recorded in China in the ninth century.

I first encountered the Jewish version of this tale in the classic collection *Yiddish Folktales*, edited by Beatrice Silverman Weinreich, under the title "How Much Do You Love Me?" According to Weinreich, the tale was collected in the 1920s by Y. L. Cahan in Smorgonie, Poland, from a storyteller named Khave Rubin. The story begins with a narrative, classified as "the love test," that appears in other world folktales and can even be seen in literary works such as Shakespeare's *King Lear*. The Yiddish version seems to be a composite of the two tale types. The song "Mazel Tov" is a traditional eastern European wedding song. According to musicologist Chana Mlotek, it was collected in Bucharest in 1955.

My grandmother Celia Cohen was born in Bialystok, a city in the southern part of Poland. She grew up speaking Polish and Russian, and was also fluent in Yiddish, the language of the Jews of eastern Europe. My great-grandmother Ida was a seamstress. On a winter's night, she would gather her children near the kitchen stove to read, to sew, and to tell stories. Every time a story is told in another language, by another teller, it changes to fit the listener and the times. The Jewish storytellers of eastern Europe gave this well-known tale their own special flavor, making it part of the greatest treasury of Yiddish lore, a *vunder-mayse*—a wonder tale—that my grandmother might have heard in her own childhood, on a cold winter's night in Bialystok.

For Sarah Bailey—Saraleh—with love always
— N. J.

To Alon, Caitlin, and Tal
with love from Grandma
—L. A.

Once upon a time in Poland, in a small town near
the city of Lublin, there lived a rabbi who had a wife and
three young daughters. The eldest daughter's name was
Reyzeleh. The middle daughter's name was Khaveleh.
And the youngest daughter's name was Mireleh.

The children grew up watching their mother in all she did. Once a week, they would help her carry sacks of flour and baskets of vegetables back from the marketplace. In time, Reyzeleh became an expert seamstress. She could sew and embroider elegant hallah covers and the most delicate tablecloths.

Khaveleh loved to sing. From morning till night, her

voice could be heard echoing through the halls of the house as she hummed a fiddler's tune or a Sabbath melody. Only Mireleh had no special gift. She spent her time daydreaming by the window. Whenever she saw her father walking up the path, she ran to greet him. The rabbi loved all his children, but he had a special place in his heart for Mireleh.

One day the rabbi found himself beset by a problem—a question he could not find the answer to. It was not written in any of his holy books. It was not discussed in the pages of the Talmud, the books of Jewish law. Still, the question kept appearing in his mind. "I know that I love my children," the rabbi said to himself, "but how much do they love me? I must discover the answer."

That evening, as Reyzeleh sat in her chair, sewing a new hallah cover, the rabbi stopped and asked her, "Reyzeleh, how much do you love me?" She replied, "Oh, Father, I love you as much as diamonds!" And he was content. Then he went to Khaveleh and asked her, "Khaveleh, my little turtledove, how much do you love me?" And she replied, "Father, I love you as much as gold and silver!" And he was happy. Finally he went to Mireleh and asked her, "Mireleh, my youngest child, my precious one, how much do you love me?" Mireleh looked straight at him and replied, "Father, I love you the way meat loves salt."

The rabbi was horrified. "What? You love me no more than salt?"

At that moment all the laws and commandments of loving-kindness flew from his head. He was so angry and hurt by her words that he drove her from the house and told her never to return.

Mireleh ran down the road, past the synagogue and the marketplace, past the walls of the town, out into the countryside. The tears ran down her cheeks like summer rain. "Where am I to go?" she wept to herself. "What am I to do?"

As she stood there, not knowing which way to turn, a stranger appeared before her. He was an old man with a long, flowing beard—yet he had the shining eyes of a gentle young man. A golden glow seemed to surround him. In one hand he carried a tall silver staff, and in the other, a small wooden stick.

The stranger spoke to Mireleh and said, "Mireleh, I know why you are running down this road, but do not fear. Dry your eyes. I am here to help you, for you have always been a kind and loving child. Now listen carefully to my words. Take the path that goes to the east, over a wooden bridge and past a grove of birch trees, until you see a large stone house. It is the home of Rabbi Yitskhok ben Levi, the renowned scholar of Lublin. He lives there with his wife and son.

"Before you leave, you must take this. It is a magic stick. All you have to do is tap it on the ground three times and anything you wish for will appear. It may help you in times of trouble. You have heard my words and you have my blessings. Now go!" And before Mireleh had time to thank him, a puff of wind blew through the air, and he disappeared.

Many hours later, when Mireleh reached the large stone house, she walked up to the window and looked inside. There was a rabbi, his wife, and their son, a tall young man. Rabbi Yitskhok was reciting the blessing over the loaves of hallah bread. Mireleh knocked softly and the rabbi came to the door. Once inside, she rushed to the kitchen, sat down by the stove, and began to cry. Her clothes were torn and her face was covered with dust and ashes. Rabbi Yitskhok and his wife and son stood around her, wondering what to do.

"Why are you crying?" the rabbi's wife asked, but Mireleh did not reply. The good woman went to the table and brought Mireleh a bowl of chicken soup. But Mireleh couldn't eat or speak; she could only sit in the corner by the stove and weep. "Well," the rabbi said, "she is poor and homeless. We must help those in need. Let her stay here. She can sleep in the attic."

Mireleh went up the stairs into the attic and closed the door behind her. The room was bare except for a straw pallet, a few rickety chairs and a broken-down table that stood on the hardwood floor. All that day she stayed in her room while Rabbi Yitskhok and his family went to the synagogue. In the evening, when they returned from Sabbath prayers, she heard the rabbi say to his wife, "Tomorrow we travel to Cracow for a wedding feast. The beggar girl we took in must stay behind."

In the morning, Mireleh watched through the window as they rode off in their carriage. "I too would like to go to the wedding," Mireleh said to herself, "but how shall I get there?" Suddenly, she remembered the magic stick. She tapped the stick three times on the floor and said, "I would like to have a dress of satin embroidered with pearls! I would like to have a garland of roses for my hair and a pair of satin slippers for my feet!" No sooner had she spoken than all those things appeared. Soon she was dressed and on her way to Cracow.

By the time she arrived, the marriage ceremony was over and the wedding celebration had begun. Musicians played on fiddle and flute, and the badkhn, the merry-making jester, was telling jokes and spinning verses in rhyme and song. Mireleh hid her stick in the folds of her dress as she stood in the doorway. As soon as she stepped into the room, the music stopped. The badkhn closed his mouth and was silent. The guests stared. Even the bride and groom stared. Who was this lovely maiden? How

had she arrived all alone? And where was her family?

Mysterious as she was, Rabbi Yitshok's son was delight-
ed to see her. Quickly he went up to her and bowed.
"Won't you have this dance with me?" Mireleh gladly
accepted. As they danced, he begged to know her name,
but she would not speak. The servants offered her food,
but she would not eat. He pleaded with her to tell him
something, anything about who she was, but she would
not say a word.

At midnight, Rabbi Yitskhok's son left the wedding
party to think over his problem. How could he find a way
to speak with this young maiden? An idea suddenly
came to him. He went outside and found a bucket, which
he filled with tar and pitch from the roadside. Then he
took a brush and covered the front steps of the house
with the contents of the bucket. As the moon rose in the
night sky, he sat by the house and waited.

It was almost dawn. Mireleh knew that she had to get
back to the attic before Rabbi Yitskhok and his family
returned home. When no one was watching, she slipped
out the door. But one of her satin slippers got stuck on
the tar and pitch that the rabbi's son had left on the steps.

Quickly Mireleh tapped her magic stick. "Take me to the house of Rabbi Yitskhok ben Levi of Lublin!" she cried. A rush of wind swirled around her, and in an instant, she was in her attic room—still wearing only one shoe.

The rabbi's son ran to the steps. He picked up the satin slipper and held it in his hand. After studying the shoe, he said to himself, "I will marry only the young woman who can wear this satin slipper!"

He set off that very day. From town to town and village to village, he traveled. Everywhere he went, he asked young maidens to try on the delicate shoe. But it didn't fit any of them.

Tired and lonely, he made his way back home to speak
to his parents.

"Mother, Father, I will marry only the one who can fit this slipper. But I cannot find her anywhere!"

Just then, Mireleh stepped out from behind the kitchen door. "Why don't you let me try it?" she asked. The rabbi's son was taken aback. "You came to us a poor beggar, covered with mud and dust. We let you stay here for tsedokeh, for the sake of charity. You could never dance in the shoes of the lovely maiden I saw at the wedding!"

Before he could say another word, Mireleh snatched the slipper from his hands and put it on. It fit perfectly. Then she reached into her pocket and pulled out the other shoe. They were a pair. The rabbi's son was astonished. Could it be true that this beggar was the maiden he had danced with?

That night, Rabbi Yitskhok and his wife both had the same dream. A traveler who had a long beard and carried a silver staff appeared before them. He spoke to each in turn and said, "Your son must keep his vow and promise, or misfortune will follow!"

The very next day, Mireleh called the rabbi's son up to the attic. "I know you are wondering about me. It is true that I came to you in rags and alone, but things are not always what they seem." She tapped her stick on the floor three times and wished for a beautiful shawl for herself and an elegant new suit for him. As soon as she spoke the words, everything she wished for appeared. The rabbi's son stared, trembling in his boots. "Do not fear this magic," Mireleh said, "for it came to me with kind words and a blessing."

The rabbi's son went back downstairs and spoke to his parents. He knew that wherever she had come from, Mireleh had been blessed with a special gift.

"Mother, Father, I am going to marry Mireleh. Everything will be all right."

And so it was decided.

A few days before the wedding, Mireleh walked into the kitchen. Six cooks were busy preparing the feast for the wedding banquet. As Mireleh walked among them, she whispered, "Don't put any salt in the food. Remember what I say, don't put any salt in the food!"

Finally the day of the wedding arrived. The guests came in carriages and coaches, on horseback and on foot. Everyone gathered in the courtyard of the synagogue for the ceremony. Rabbi Yitskhok's son stood under the huppah, the wedding canopy, and Mireleh was led down the aisle to stand with him. She was dressed in a shimmering gown, and on her feet she wore a pair of satin slippers. Her face was covered with an embroidered lace veil.

The bride and groom exchanged rings and spoke the words that would bind them together as husband and wife. Rabbi Yitskhok himself pronounced the seven blessings over the bridal couple. At the end of the prayers and blessings, the groom stepped on the wine glass. Then Mireleh lifted up her veil. "Mazel tov!" cried all the guests. "Mazel tov!" cried Rabbi Yitskhok and his wife.

When the dancing was over, the guests sat down to enjoy the feast. Mireleh walked among them to make sure they were happy and content. The light from flickering torches cast shadows on the merrymakers as the sun slowly set and evening stars appeared in the sky. One of the guests, a visiting rabbi, was tasting the food with scowls and grimaces. Mireleh came and spoke to him. "I can see you are troubled, sir. Is there anything wrong with the dishes we have prepared?"

"This food tastes terrible! It has no salt!" the rabbi said. In the half-light of shadow and flame, the bride gazed at the worn face and wrinkled brow. She knew the face well. "But, Father," Mireleh whispered, "don't you remember? I told you I loved you the way meat loves salt and you drove me from your house!"

As soon as the rabbi recognized his daughter, he fainted dead away. The guests threw rosewater on his face and put a bottle of smelling salts under his nose. When he revived, he hugged and embraced her. How he had missed his Mireleh all this time! "My daughter, forgive me!" he wept. "You spoke only words of truth to me, as you have always done." Then Reyzeleh and Khaveleh came running to her side, as did her mother. At last, the family was reunited.

At that moment, an old man with the shining eyes of youth appeared before them, carrying a silver staff in his hand. Mireleh ran to greet the old man, for she knew him at last. This was Elijah the Prophet, who descends from heaven to help those in need. Then Elijah smiled and waved his staff over the bridal couple. But once again, before Mireleh could thank him he was gone.

Mireleh and the rabbi's son lived together in honor and contentment for many years. As for the magic wooden stick, when Mireleh's own children were born, she broke it in two and gave one half to each daughter, for good fortune should always be shared. Though the stick has long since disappeared, the blessings of Elijah can stay with us always, as long as we care for each other, from one generation to the next, with kind and loving hearts.

And so the story's ended,
Like honey from a cup,
Their happiness brimmed over—
We'll sip each droplet up.

MAZEL TOV!

Vivo ♩ = 148

Ma - zel tov un ma - zel tov. Oy, freyt zikh yi - dn, freyt!

Gi - kher, oy, gi - kher, di khu - pe z'on - ge - greyt!

Der fe - ter Yo - sye un di mu - me Zi - se - le

veln geyn a hop - ke, un shteln a fi - se - le, oy!

Ma - zel tov un ma - zel tov. Oy, freyt zikh yi - dn, freyt!

Gi - kher, oy, gi - kher, di khu - pe z'on - ge - greyt!

Fregt nit keyn sha - le, ot geyt di ka - le.

Freyt zikh, yi - dn, in a gu - ter sho!

Mazel tov, Mazel tov.

Rejoice, dear Jews, rejoice!

The huppah is ready, the relatives are coming.

Hurry, hurry, here comes the bride!

Be merry and let us wish the couple happiness.

DATE DUE
